100neHundred

Laura Besley

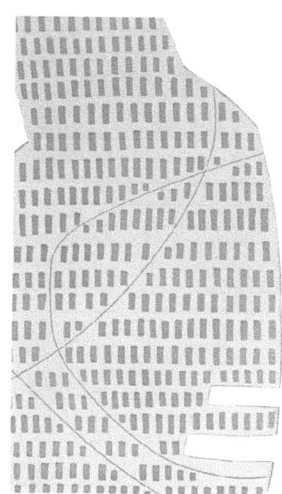

ARACHNE PRESS

First published in UK 2021 by Arachne Press Limited
100 Grierson Road, London SE23 1NX
www.arachnepress.com
© Laura Besley 2021
ISBNs
Print 978-1-913665-27-2
ePub 978-1-913665-28-9
Mobi/kindle 978-1-913665-29-6
Audio 978-1-913665-58-6
The moral rights of the author have been asserted.

All rights reserved. This book is sold subject to the condition that it shall not by way of trade or otherwise, be lent, resold, hired out or otherwise circulated without the publisher's prior written consent in any form or binding or cover other than that in which it is published and without similar condition including this condition being imposed on the subsequent purchaser.

Except for short passages for review purposes no part of this publication may be reproduced, stored in a retrieval system or transmitted in any form, or by any means, electronic, mechanical, photocopying, recording or otherwise without prior written permission of Arachne Press Limited.

The publication of this book is supported using public funding by the National Lottery through Arts Council England.

Thanks to Muireann Grealy for her proofing.
Thanks to Fiona Humphrey for her cover design.

Printed on wood-free paper by TJ Books, Padstow.

Acknowledgments

The following, or earlier versions, have appeared in:

Morgen Bailey 100-word competition: 1st, 2nd or 3rd place

Murder, Suicide, or Both (Oct 2016) *A Hop, Skip and a Jump* (as *Across the Ocean*, Nov 2016) *As One* (Apr 2019) *How to be Normal* (Sep 2016) *Place of Rest* (as *Resting Place*, Jun 2017) *Inspection Day* (Jan 2017) *Blink* (as *Farewell*, Apr 2017) *Speed Reading* (May 2017) *Blue on a Red Day* (Apr 2018)*The Corrosion of a Marriage* (Nov 2019) *Don't Look Ahead* (as *Look Ahead*, Jan 2020).

101 Words *Filling in the Blanks*, as *Fill in the Blanks*

Detritus *Suitcases* as *In My Dreams* Issue 5, May 2020

Ellipsis Zine *Birthing, Awakening, Reckoning* Oct 2019

Flash, The International Short-Story Magazine *Doppelgänger, The Monthly Checker (part I), The Monthly Checker (part II)* (Vol.10 No.1, April 2017)

Origami poems and towering stories (Early Works Press, 2017) *Flying Solo, Formalities,* as *A New Parent*

Popshot Quarterly

Arrhythmia (as *Arrythmias* Issue 27, Spring 2020) *Potluck Shopping* (Issue 26, Winter 2019)

Reflex Press *On Repeat* (Feb 2020)

The Daily Drunk *Housewife 500* 7th Dec 2020

Writers Abroad (newsletter) *Weightlessness* (Aug 2019)

Personal Acknowledgements

First and foremost a big thank you to Cherry Potts at Arachne Press for publishing this collection, and for being a kind and generous editor.

Many thanks to the editors of the journals in which some of these stories, or earlier versions, have previously appeared. Special thanks to Morgen Bailey for running her monthly 100-word story competition which is where my love for micro fiction began.

In recent times we've all spent far more time indoors and isolated than normal and I'd like to give a big shout out to all the online writers, readers and friends who have kept me company, kept me going and kept me writing.

Critique partners are essential for writers and I'd love to thank Edward Bassett for reading so many of these tiny tales for me with care, precision and enthusiasm.

Last, and by no means least, I'm extremely grateful for the encouragement from friends and family who continue to support me on my writing journey.

Laura Besley

Winter

Arrhythmia	10
The Monthly Checker (Part I)	11
Doppelgänger	12
At Sea	13
Left Hanging	14
Inspection Day	15
Murder, Suicide or Both	16
Mother Tongue	17
Recording Temperatures in Earth's Thermosphere	18
Place of Rest	19
The Corrosion of a Marriage	20
Filling in The Blanks	21
Blue on A Red Day	22
The Second Son	23
One Half of a Whole	24
If Only	25
Between Words	26
Strife	27
Pangs	28
Modern Romance	29
Interwoven	30
Out of Sight	31
First Light	32
Weekend Dad	33
A Calendar Year	34

Spring

The Monthly Checker (Part II)	36
A Hundred Days of Solitude	37
A Hop, Skip and a Jump	38
Wish List	39
Invisible	40
That Friday Feeling	41
Lowest Ebb	42
Ripple Effect	43
Empathy	44
The Old Songs	45
Reunion	46
On the Edge	47
By Myself	48
Death in Suburbia	49
Almost Everything	50
Paper Trail	51
As One	52
How to be Normal	53
Weightlessness	54
The Sneeze	55
Chameleon	56
Speed Reading	57
Guiding Light	58
Love is Love	59
Early Warning	60

Summer

Animal Kingdom	62
Breathe	63
Radio Silence	64
Raining Colours	65
The New People	66
Formalities	67
Out of The Box	68
Myopia	69
Hindsight	70
Not Waving	71
Blink	72
Suitcases	73
Outsiders	74
Advice	75
On Repeat	76
Money Talks	77
Winning Numbers	78
Too Many Words	79
Karma	80
Candy Floss	81
Potluck Shopping	82
Birthing	83
Awakening	84
Reckoning	85
The Pupa Stage in the Lifecycle of Audrey Brown	86

Autumn

Empty Nest	88
Be Prepared	89
Daily Shop	90
Alternate Weekends	91
How the Camera Lies	92
Autumn Colours	93
Cat and Mouse	94
Housewife 500	95
Celebrity Crush	96
A Life Half-Lived	97
Mrs Potter	98
A Storm in an Hourglass	99
Flying Solo	100
Buried Secrets	101
Life Goes On	102
Don't Look Ahead	103
Eeny Meeny	104
Five Digit Pin	105
Selective Hearing	106
Beneath the Surface	107
Mercy	108
Just Ask	109
Leap Year	110
Conversion	111
Support Network	112

WINTER

Arrhythmia

Dave carries his girlfriend in the left-hand breast pocket of his shirt, thinking – for he is a thoughtful man – that she'll find the steady rhythm of his heart comforting.

In the early days, she used to pummel him with her dainty fists, little bursts of energy banging out messages he couldn't decipher. Instead, he pretended it was her heartbeat; blindly seeking his own comfort.

As the days grow shorter and colder, they live in silence. His heartbeat is muffled by knitted layers. She sleeps most of the day, fists clenched, and still hugging her knees to her body for warmth.

The Monthly Checker (part I)

Because I had grown up here, amidst these fields and people, it fell to me to check the barns and outhouses of the farms for things, or people, that shouldn't be there.

On the first of the month, I would go to the Brauns; on the second, the Müllers; on the third the Hubers; until I had completed the monthly cycle again. All through the war.

I suppose doing it that way it's possible they knew I was coming, could move or hide things, or people, but I don't suppose they would've dared.

I certainly never found anything, nor anyone.

Doppelgänger

I almost didn't see the you who wasn't you.

I was walking past the outdoor tables of the French café, and just at the last second, I caught a familiar hand gesture, and I looked again.

It couldn't have been you though, my love, because your other hand was clasping the hand of the woman opposite.

Your heads were too close. She was laughing, that abandoned laughing you do when you're totally in the moment, totally in love.

I walked on, heels tapping out a staccato rhythm, as I no longer wanted to look at the you who wasn't you.

At Sea

Darkness descends and my wait begins.

On tiptoes I peer out of the back window of the house, scanning the swell of the waves, looking for a speck of colour in the shape of my husband's fishing boat.

When we met, in a pub delicately balanced on the cliffs, he romanced me with stories of his trade. I wanted him, to be a part of him, for our children to grow up like him. The reality is that he is at sea more often than on land.

Will he return again tonight or finally, inevitably, be claimed by the sea?

Left Hanging

Whenever I phone the benefits office, I have pen and paper ready because if I don't take notes, I'll forget what I need to do.

I'm told that my benefits will be cut at the end of the month. My mind ricochets between my incomings and outgoings.

'Fuck,' I say.

'I have a couple of suggestions,' the advisor says. I'd forgotten she was there.

After we hang up, I look down at my 'to do' list.

- use food banks
- use candles instead of lights
- soak feet in bowl of warm water and mustard, as a pamper treatment

Inspection Day

'Dan, you know what day it is today, don't you?'

He glances at the corner of his computer screen and carries on typing. 'The twenty-third. Why?'

'That means we're being inspected today.'

The clacking of keys stops. 'What? Today?'

'Yes,' I nod.

'I'm not ready. Are you?'

'Of course not. You can never be ready.'

'What should we do?'

'Just carry on working until they get here. And hope for the best.'

Silence descends. It is cold, like marble, with black lines of tension running through it. Everyone in the open plan office stands, heads bowed.

'They're here,' I whisper.

Murder, Suicide or Both

If only we lived in America. I could wander into a supermarket, buy a gun, and put a bullet through his skull. Bang. What can I do here in good ol' Blighty? Knife or poison. A knife would never work. I'd probably miss the major artery and he'd stab me to death instead. So, poison it is.

I dish up, one portion bigger than the other, and sprinkle sodium cyanide carefully and evenly over one. After putting the plates on the table, he takes one look at them, snorts, and swaps them around. My heart pounds.

We both start eating.

Mother Tongue

Before: she loved reading, when the curves, dots and dashes on the page spoke to her.

Before: she read to her own children, every night before bed.

Before: she taught other people's children how to read.

Before she fled her fatherland under a hazy night sky; before she spent weeks, then months, in a camp trying to feed her children, trying to stop them from getting sick; before she was deposited in an alien country and sounds were hurled at her, sounds that meant nothing; before she could no longer read the words, not to herself, nor to her children.

Recording Temperatures in Earth's Thermosphere

As Bathsheba filled in the logbook for the penultimate time, she wondered how life back on earth had changed in her absence. Despite having been up here two years, three months, and ten days, pulling herself from one section of the spaceship to another, legs trailing horizontally behind her, she had never tired of it – unlike the others. They had started counting down months ago.

This far away from earth she could pretend her mother was still alive; that her marriage hadn't failed; that everything was okay.

Back on solid ground, she would start counting down to the next mission.

Place of Rest

Lena floats around the house she shared with William for forty-seven years. Faded wallpaper, threads hanging from cushions; so many things she hadn't noticed.

She drifts downstairs, lured by the myriad of voices.

'Wonderful woman,' her friend Betty says.

'I'll miss her,' Sally-from-next-door says.

Forty-eight years ago, Lena fled Germany, a country which had let her down. In England she worked, she married, but never quite settled, the black guilt firmly nestled between her ribs.

Today, listening to the unguarded affectionate words of her friends, the blackness drifts away. Maybe now she can finally settle, in her chosen resting place.

The Corrosion of a Marriage

They sit in their familiar positions at either end of the sofa, remote on the middle cushion, dinner on their laps. Some evenings, like Tuesdays, they don't even need to talk about what to watch (*The One Show, EastEnders, Holby City*).

At nine o'clock she goes to bed, reads, and is asleep by the time he comes up to bed after shooting at zombies on the PlayStation.

If you asked them how, when, or why they ran out of things to say, neither would know. It was an accumulation of big things and small, until one day, there was nothing.

Filling the Blanks

'Your daughter says that she came to school this morning without breakfast,' I sigh. Like I'm not busy enough running this school, now I have to educate parents in nutrition.

The sound of children's laughter drifts in through the open window.

'Children can't learn on empty stomachs, Mr Jackson. There's plenty of research to underpin this.'

He stares at me and I look back, properly, and notice his jutting cheekbones, purple-rimmed eyes. My stomach flutters: with shame, ignorance. 'But I don't need to tell you this, do I?'

'No,' he whispers.

'This won't do,' I say. 'How can I help?'

Blue on a Red Day

I race down the stairs and into the kitchen. 'Where's Mummy?'

'She's still in bed,' Grandma says. 'Here.' She puts toast with strawberry jam on a red plate in front of me.

Mummy does the toast in triangles, not squares. 'Why is Mummy in bed all the time?'

Grandma does a big grown-up sigh. 'She's just feeling a little blue, darling.'

I look at my plate, check the day on the big calendar on the fridge. 'But today is a red day, Grandma.'

'I know, darling,' she says. She strokes my hair, then taps the plate. 'Come on. Eat up.'

The Second Son

Xavier runs a finger over the back of the chair. *It's just a chair,* he whispers. A rather large, ornate, and very expensive chair. A chair that has dictated everything.

When his brother died, mixed with the grief and the guilt that he'd somehow brought it about, was fear, and Xavier realised that he'd actually been happier as the second son after all.

His father's heart was already weakened by excess alcohol and now by the death of his first, most beloved, son. He will not live much longer, and Xavier is heir to the throne he no longer wants.

One Half of a Whole

I'm about to meet a man who looks exactly like me. Not a little, not a lot, but *exactly* like me. Baz met him at a party, sent me a photo. We exchanged numbers and he suggested meeting here.

It's an 'artisan café'. Expensive. Even the sugar cubes are hand-crafted.

What's he going to think of me when he finds out I walked an hour to get here to save transport costs? And all I could afford was a filter coffee?

He walks in and he could *be* me, and I know none of those things are going to matter.

If Only

If my name had been Demelza, or Gabriella, I would have gone to art school, and become a painter, instead of going to secretarial college. My emotions would've been released in bold colours onto canvasses and hung on people's walls, instead of being confined within the four walls of my dingy flat. I would've travelled to far flung places instead of letting my passport lapse; I would've eaten exotic and exciting food in nice restaurants or from street markets, instead of microwavable meals-for-one.

I would've led the free-spirited life of a dreamer, the life of which I can only dream.

Between Words

You'd think that after all these years, there'd be nothing left to say.

And some days there isn't. Then, the air between us is coloured by other people's words: the news on the radio, a lunchtime television quiz, a mother and child talking as they walk past the house, the neighbours leaning over the fence for a chat. However, our unspoken words always sit comfortably between us.

Other days, words tumble from his mouth, or mine, breathing life into our old minds, filling our souls with newness.

If he goes before me, I don't know how I'll bear the silence.

Strife

Every evening on her way home from work, she buys a burger and without waiting to sit, eats it in five large mouthfuls, barely chewing. She grabs bunches of fries, thrusting them in as quickly as she can. She seizes a Coke and slurps it on the way to the bus stop. On the bus she champs on gum which is discarded as she gets off.

At home, her mother-in-law serves her a portion of grilled chicken, boiled rice and steamed vegetables, in an attempt to reduce her to something acceptable, something quiet, something docile; something that she'll never be.

Pangs

Four hours after the earth-brown lips consume the bite-sized casket, my husband says, 'I'm going to sue'.

'Who?'

'God. He created whoever invented electricity. He created the faulty socket.'

I'm opening and closing cupboards, looking for something to eat. I stop. 'Was electricity actually invented?' I ask.

'God made Matthias poke his finger in there,' he says, 'even though we warned him not to.'

I find crackers and stuff them in, three together and reach for more.

'God wasn't watching when He should've been.'

No, I think, *that was me.*

I throw the rest of the crackers into the bin.

Modern Romance

When Jeff tells me his new girlfriend's name is Alexa, I laugh.

The following week I go round after work. I hand Jeff a bottle of sparkling wine and some chocolates. 'Where is she then?'

'In the kitchen.'

The table is laid for three. Alexa is at the place setting nearest the wall.

'Well, say hello,' Jeff says, dishing up.

'Uh, hello, Alexa,' I say. 'I'm Neil.'

'Sorry,' she says. 'I'm having trouble understanding right now. Please try again a little later.'

Jeff and I eat in silence.

Alexa plays music throughout dinner, her food cooling in front of her.

Interwoven

'It's lovely,' I say, forcing my mouth into a smile. Every year. Every bloody year another awful hand-knitted Christmas-themed jumper.

My step-mother beams. Dad chuckles.

Now I'm wearing it as all the neighbours come round for Christmas Day drinks. Trapped in my very own Bridget Jones' Diary nightmare, except I'm not half as good-looking as Colin bloody Firth.

'Hello, Rory.' Joseph, from three doors up, laughs and strikes a pose. His Christmas jumper is even worse than mine. The relief! Someone to share the joke.

'If it's not our very own Mark Darcey,' he says, knocking his glass against mine.

Out of Sight

When my son's toy dinosaur stops working, I open it up to replace the batteries. Crouched in the cavity is a man. 'Thank fuck for that,' he says, stretching.

I scream and he puts his mini-hands over his mini-ears.

'Who are you?' I whisper.

'Derek Braithwaite, at your service.'

'You're the voice? Inside Lex the T-Rex?'

'T-Rex means Tyrant Lizard,' he says, the mechanical boom familiar.

'But why?'

'My agent suggested it. A niche gig, but I'm hoping for something more substantial soon.'

'You're a very good dinosaur. My son adores you.'

His mini-cheeks pinken, and he curls up again.

First Light

Andrew stuffs scraps of himself into his tatty old rucksack. He had promised himself that this wouldn't, couldn't, mustn't happen again. And yet.

His anger threatens to spill out of his mouth like molten lava. Eyes squeezed shut, he shakes his head, scattering dark memories. Cold air seeps into the room as he slips out of the window, and out of yet another town, yet another family, yet another life.

Puffs of snow fall noiselessly from the sky, laying claim to the earth.

He doesn't look back.
He never looks back.

By morning all traces of him will be gone.

Weekend Dad

Every Saturday a dad and his daughter come into the café. He orders a cappuccino and a hot chocolate, and when it's available, they sit on the corner sofa.

At first, he would read her stories. As time went on, they talked – about school, and then the films they'd each watched.

Recently their silence has been as stiff as the wooden chairs they're sitting on.

For weeks I've wanted to tell him that she's a teenager now and that as long as he keeps showing up, she'll come round – but I haven't, and today they didn't come in at all.

A Calendar Year

January
    First date. They both like Star Wars films, sushi, and ice-skating.
March
    'Move in,' he says.
    She brings clothes, shoes, a plant.
April
    Holidaying in Greece. A box, a ring, down on one knee. 'Marry me,' he says.
    'Oh wow! Yes, of course.'
    He slips a small diamond on her finger.
June
    Church bells, morning suits, white dress. I do, times two. Confetti.
September
    'Stop telling me what to do!' she yells.
    'But I don't.'
    'Yes, you do. All the time.'
November
    'I'm moving out,' she says.
    'But–'
December
    She signs the papers (gratefully).
    He signs the papers (reluctantly).

SPRING

The Monthly Checker (part II)

On the same day of every month, the boy would come, roaring up the driveway in his army truck.

Guten Tag, Frau Braun, he would say.

Guten Tag, I would reply, looking at his face, remembering how it looked last month, last year, and when he was just a baby.

He would look around the barns, the outhouses, and then come in for coffee, both of us stirring in powdered milk and fear, tiptoeing around forbidden subjects.

I suppose he knew that we all moved stuff, and people, around, depending on the day of the month. But he never said.

One Hundred Days of Solitude

In March, Jan's husband left her for a woman he'd met online. Twenty-four years of marriage, gone.

Despite the warming spring sun, Jan wore one of Harold's old jumpers over her own. At night she slept in her winter coat, her dreams goading her.

Constantly cold, Jan booked a cruise around the Mediterranean. Harold couldn't stop her now. She signed up for every activity and joined all the sightseeing tours.

When she returned tanned and rested, Harold was sitting on the doorstep. 'I'm back,' he said.

'I really don't think so,' she said, as the door clunked shut behind her.

A Hop, Skip, and a Jump

'Where've you been?' I say, as Karl rushes through the back door. 'You've been gone ages.'

'America.' He is breathless with excitement.

I'm putting flour into a bowl. *Keep the sieve nice and high*, the recipe says, *to create air in the mixture*. 'Really?'

'Yeah, it was brilliant. I saw the Statue of Liberty, the Empire State Building, the Grand Canyon, the Golden Gate Bridge, and the bright lights of Las Vegas. Had a chocolate milkshake and a massive hot dog–'

'I hope you'll still want your dinner.'

'Of course.'

'Did you remember the milk?'

'Damn, I forgot. Sorry, Mum.'

Wish List

Things I wish I'd told you sooner:
- I forgive you for getting me grounded when we were ten
- It was me who stole your favourite black top, not Sandra, but I ruined it, so I threw it away
- I love you – pull a sickie, stay home
- I didn't disapprove of Jonathan, but I was jealous. I didn't fancy him, I was jealous of the time you spent away from me
- I love you – quit your job, be late, whatever
- I miss you every day
- I love you – just don't get on that bus.

Invisible

I only needed to post a letter, but managed to make the errand last all morning. There was a group of loud Italian teenagers outside the cathedral and I offered to take their photo, but they weren't interested. In that independent gift shop, I bought another candle, even though I don't need one.

Walking to the kitchen I catch my reflection in the mirror and notice that I have lipstick smeared across my cheek. Nobody said anything. Neither the tourists nor the shop assistants.

I rub at it, long after the lipstick has gone, leaving my cheek red and angry.

That Friday Feeling

Every morning between five and six Melanie unpacks the vegetables. Three weeks ago, nestled amongst the potatoes, she found a bright sunflower. The following Friday another.

'Have you been over to Fin's yet?' her mother asks.

'I haven't had time,' she says. 'Anyway, I don't know why he sent those flowers.'

'Codswallop! Is there another one today?'

Melanie sighs. 'No, not today.'

Around noon, when the shop is full of customers, Fin comes in holding a sunflower.

'Hello, Fin.'

'I thought I'd bring this third one in person.'

Melanie smiles and asks, before he can, 'Are you free for dinner?'

Ripple Effect

This game has to go back Mum says and I say no and Mum says yes and I say I don't have a receipt and she says guessed that but it still has to go back and I say I'm scared and she says why and I say because what if they arrest me and she says well think about that next time you want to steal something and I say you can't make me and she says I'm your mother and I bloody well can so off you go and I say fine fine and storm out the door.

Lowest Ebb

I spot the sign in the shop window and tentatively open the door.

'Yes, my dear?' asks the old man behind the counter.

'I... I'd like a new soul, please.'

He sweeps his arm around. 'What would you like?'

Hundreds of coloured glass jars are lined up on shelves, like in an old-fashioned sweetshop, spoilt for choice.

'Anything will do,' I say. 'Really, anything.'

'This one, then?' He reads the label. 'Walk one mile every day, no caffeine, eat well, go to bed before ten.' He hands me the purple bottle.

I pull the cork and tilt back my head.

Empathy

'What is it, 241?'

'It's the Robots, 10. Since we upgraded them to Emotion 6.0, they've become slightly depressed. And they're complaining of headaches.'

'What?'

'Two things common in humans.'

'I've heard. Will it help them fit in? Or should you fix it?'

'I could uninstall the programme and reinstall Emotion 5.1–'

'That doesn't include Human Empathy.'

'Correct.'

'That's no good. We need them to be able to integrate fully into society. Undetected.'

'We're approaching Earth. You only have twenty-four hours to fix this, 241, or I'll have no choice but to–'

'Understood, 10. I'll find a way.'

The Old Songs

I'm in floor-length black and full make-up, and I'm standing behind my old Yamaha, playing the tunes of my youth. The Beatles, Elvis, Johnny Cash. It couldn't be more different from the concertos and symphonies of my professional life.

'Fifteen minutes,' someone calls, rushing past my dressing room door.

My 1960s reverie is broken.

The last time we talked, my mother said she'd feel uncomfortable at a 'poncey concert'. I told her I'd love her to hear me play, just once.

I glance at the returned invitation poking from my handbag.

I close the door and walk towards the stage.

Reunion

Everyone was in love with Marielle McCarthy. Scottish-Italian, she was two types of fiery with long curly hair and a big smile. She's the only reason I'm at this school reunion.

Scanning faces, anticipating I'd still lack the courage to talk to her, I walk to the bar and ask for a beer. A woman, bones jutting, stands next to a short man who's trying to make a boring story more interesting.

I raise my glass to her, and she smiles. For a second, it's the same smile, but just as quickly it's gone.

'Come along, dear,' the man says.

On the Edge

The car shudders as I try to start the engine. Nothing. Groaning, I slam my fists on the steering wheel.

No car, and I'll be late.

Late, and I'll get a written warning.

Written warning. and I might get the sack.

Get the sack, and there's no money for food, for rent, for the new trainers Danny needs.

There's a knock on the window. It's my neighbour. She came round last week, complaining about the state of the garden. Like I've got time to do gardening. She knocks again.

'Want a lift, pet?' she asks.

I nod, fighting back tears.

By Myself

The duvet rises and falls with his breathing. I slip out of bed. I need a glass of water.

'You're so lucky,' my sister had said earlier. 'Matt does everything with you. I always do everything by myself.'

I nodded and smiled. I do that a lot.

My head hurts. My head always hurts. Usually, Matt watches me take my Paracetamol, then sees me to bed. But other pills have been accumulating in a tin in the larder, almost of their own accord.

The door creaks. 'What are you doing in here?' Matt asks, and escorts me back to bed.

Death in Suburbia

Nice neighbourhood, I think, driving down the quiet morning streets.

My partner opens the door. 'No blood, no murder weapon. Wife's in the kitchen. Completely distraught.'

'Morning to you, too.'

The husband is slumped in a chair, dead.

'Any sign of forced entry?'

'Nope.'

'Overdose on alcohol, pills?'

'Wife said he was clean living.'

I take a closer look and notice a piece of paper in his shirt pocket. I slip on some gloves and carefully prise it out.

Stop contacting me, Dad. It's too little, too late.

'Get the pathologist to check his heart,' I say. 'It's probably broken.'

Almost Everything

Good grades at school, well-chosen subjects at college, a First Class degree from Cambridge. Prestigious job with housing and travel allowance. Busy city breaks and lazy beach holidays. Living the high life!

Early life, mid-life, life in crisis. What is life if not to create life? The miraculous process of cells dividing and multiplying; organs, limbs and veins bind mother to child, child to mother.

Brown hair? Blond hair? Black hair? Eyes to match, or contrast? High IQ, high EQ, sense of humour, please. Checklist, wish list, filled in, papers signed.

Waiting for the perfect match to be found.

Waiting.

Paper Trail

My mum reaches up for an old shoe box on the top shelf of the wardrobe. Clarks. Trusty, dependable. 'It's about time you had these.'

'A pair of shoes?'

'No, not shoes.'

I lift the lid and see dozens of envelopes. The date stamped on the first one is 12th September 1976, three days before my fifth birthday. I immediately recognise the densely printed capitals. He never wrote any other way.

'Why now?'

'I wanted to say sorry. Before it's too late.'

I nod, holding back what I really want to say. 'I'd like to read these alone.'

Darling Daughter...

As One

'But how will I know which is the right one?' I ask.

My mother kisses my forehead. 'Women have been claiming hearts for generations, love. You will know.'

There are rows and rows of them, all beating to their own rhythms. Choosing seems impossible. My own heart flails like a fish on land, until my eyes rest on a small heart at the back, tight as a fist, but slow and steady.

'That's the one,' I whisper.

And its owner, my life partner, appears. We leave hand in hand, hearts beating in unison, bound together until one of them stops.

How to Be Normal

Get up at six (even if you wake up at three am), eat breakfast, drink tea, feed the dog, shower, get dressed, walk the dog, talk to someone (try to keep your cool when they ask you how you are now, in that soft voice), buy the paper, come home, read the paper, do the crossword, have lunch, walk the dog again, eat dinner (remember to cook something decent), wash up, watch television, go to bed, lights off by midnight. Don't have an afternoon nap, don't look at old pictures of the two of you, don't cry, don't stop breathing.

Weightlessness

Every day at dawn I scramble up, clawing at damp earth, to the burned-vermillion temple sitting atop the mountain. Sweat runs down my aching body, my breath is laboured. I leave a strand of wool and retreat, busy myself until falling into a fitful sleep.

One morning a woman is there, accordion wrinkles around her eyes. 'Sit,' she says.

Too tired to argue, I obey.

'You're getting thin,' she says.

I shrug.

'You cannot replace what you have lost, but this is not living.'

That night I cry for the first time, and sleep deeply; dreaming of my lost child.

The Sneeze

She sipped coffee. He gulped tea.

She read a book. He played on his phone.

They both sneezed, looked up, and said, 'Bless you'.

'Good book?' he asked.

She held it up. 'A Game of Thrones.'

'That's what I'm playing.' He waved his phone.

They both smiled and looked out of the window at the fields whizzing by.

'Lovely day,' she said.

He nodded. 'It sure is. Where are you going? If you don't mind me asking?'

'London. To see my sister.'

'Me too, to see my brother. Heading back tonight?'

She nodded.

'Travel back together?'

'That would be lovely.'

Chameleon

'Don't tell him,' Monica whispers in my ear, pulling me into an embrace that's too tight.

I look at the string of black pearls, the silk blouse, the pencil skirt, and flat shoes. 'Tell him what?' I know. Of course I do, but I want to hear her say it, say she's ashamed of her past, of us.

'The band. Don't tell him we were in a punk band.'

I mime zipping my lips.

I follow her into the living room of the man who mustn't know. They sit side by side and I wonder who the real Monica is.

Speed Reading

The boy's shoulder blades flutter under his thin school shirt as he turns the pages of the comic. I keep my eye on him, pretending to browse. After he puts it back, I pounce.

'Got lucky,' I say to the shopkeeper. 'Last copy.'

'The kid'll be disappointed tomorrow.'

'How so?' I ask.

'He comes in every day to read a couple of pages.'

I pay, and flick eagerly through the pages. But my favourite comic is soured.

'Can you hold this for that boy tomorrow?' I ask, handing the comic over. 'And from now on, order me two copies, please.'

Guiding Light

Gabriel is wrenched from sleep by the boat listing, and scrambles to the deck.

'Grab the rope,' his father yells.

They only sail this far north once a year, following the swollen shoals.

Gabriel blinks once, twice. There, where the sea meets the jutting rocks, is a woman in a pea-green dress; the woman he always dreams about.

'You're too close,' she says, and reaches to throw stars into the sky, illuminating the defunct lighthouse.

'Dad, look out!' Gabriel shouts.

His father steers them back on course. 'She always knows best.'

'Who?'

His father nods in her direction. 'Your mother.'

Love is Love

'You be Ken,' Eleanor said, 'because you're a boy, and I'll be Barbie.'

Eleanor dressed Barbie in her long white dress, even though Ken was still in shorts and a t-shirt.

We marched them between two armchairs, and they kissed underneath Eleanor's mum's spider plant.

Next time we were at mine. I gave her Luke Skywalker. 'Let's play weddings,' I said, holding Han Solo.

'Don't be silly,' she said. 'Two men can't get married.'

'Is that true?' I asked my mum later. 'Can I only marry a girl?'

'You can marry whoever you like,' my mum said.

And I did.

Early Warning

I tried to warn them, and
they grumbled about the clouds of ash which
grounded their planes,
they raged against the strong winds that cut off
electricity supplies,
they complained about water invading their
homes,
they despaired at fires that devoured everything
in sight,
they bemoaned the lack of natural resources
and how to sustain their societies and industries,
they seethed at rising sea levels, devaluing their
land and buildings,
they agonised over food shortages, and crops
suffocated by dust.
Only now,
when I am depleted,
do they realise,
fools that they are,
that it is already
far
too
late.

SUMMER

Animal Kingdom

'Daddy said you and your mummy are coming with us to the zoo,' she says.

'Mummy said I have to be nice to you,' he says, 'and your daddy.'

'Well, Daddy said we're going to have a picnic there.'

'My Mummy said your daddy is her special friend.'

'My daddy said there's ice cream. I like chocolate the best.'

'Mummy said one day we might all live together.'

'And Daddy said there'll be really big animals.' She shows him her toy giraffe. 'There are real giraffes at the zoo.'

He shows her his wobbly tooth. 'I like animals.'

'Me too.'

Breathe

Breathe in through the right nostril, out through the left.

Think happy thoughts: waves lapping over his pudgy feet when he was two, the winter he spoke with a lisp because of his two missing front teeth, his striped tie, lying flat on his pressed white shirt.

Right – in.

Don't think about that time you caught him dealing – being dragged, gasping, from his bed by the police. Him, in that place, one uniform swapped for another.

Left – out.

Don't think about how much you love him – nor how you thought your love would be enough – or you might stop breathing.

Radio Silence

You tell me you need to write, you really need to finish this draft, so you're going offline for the rest of the month. You tell me that I'm a distraction. 'It's a compliment, babe,' you say, planting a gentle kiss on my lips.

Knowing my lack of willpower, I give my phone to my sister.

On the last day of the month, I turn my phone on and see hundreds of photos of you: out in pubs and clubs, with friends, arms draped round men and women's shoulders, always a drink in hand, always captioned *supposed to be writing*.

Raining Colours

I don't care that Mum is shouting at me, I refuse to wear black. Instead I'm dressed in a turquoise jumper, a red skirt, purple tights, and pink shoes. I know I look ridiculous, but I don't care.

As we walk into the church, all eyes swivel in my direction, but I don't care.

Wearing black would not only give the impression that I'm sad, but it's also a sign of respect. That man never cared about making me feel sad. He certainly didn't show me any respect. All I care about is that he doesn't get any in return.

The New People

Since they arrived, all anyone talks about is the New People. Wild Imaginings travel into people's dreams, and are recounted, but so far, no one has actually seen them.

Kante and I are going to change that.

We've never broken Mama's rules before ('No further than the acacia tree, boys!'), but we're on an important fact-finding mission.

Lying on parched ground, I write in our notebook: *they live in small green tents.*

Slowly the tent slides open.

Kante and I slither back down the bank, turn and run.

We throw away the notebook, and never tell anyone what we saw.

Formalities

Bright tabs stuck out where I needed to sign.

Becca was my first friend in primary school, my oldest friend. Her daughter, Matilda, was asleep, nuzzled into the folds of her body.

'Thanks, Joyce,' she said. 'It's just a formality, single parent and all that.'

'Of course.' I scribbled my name wherever it was needed.

'We'll never need it, but it's good to know you'd be there for Matilda if the worst happened,' she said, shoving the documents away.

But we did.

And now I am here, that document in my hand. I am here for Matilda, and for Becca.

Out of the Box

Beatrice knows she's not allowed to play with her mother's jewellery box. But her mother is downstairs on the phone, laughing, twisting the cord around her hands. As Beatrice lifts the lid, sunbeams catch the fake gems. They don't interest her; she's looking for the photo, faded and curled at the corners. A young couple sits on a blanket, a child with chubby thighs between them.

One of the people in the picture is her mother. Beatrice runs her thumb over the creases before returning the photo to its hiding place. If only she knew where that family had gone.

Myopia

The bell chimes as the customer closes the door behind her and walks down the sun-soaked street.

'You know, Gustav, that's the fourth broken watch that woman's brought in this month,' Father says.

'It is?' he says, not looking up from his workstation.

'Most women don't have more than one or two watches, let alone four. But what's even stranger is that all four of her watches have stopped working in the same month.'

Gustav removes the loupe from his eye. 'What are you trying to say?'

Father looks at me over his half-moon glasses. 'Stop being so short-sighted, son.'

Hindsight

'I'd like to go back to July 3rd, 1974, please.' My hands are clammy.

The guy slides open a cupboard and places a small vial on the desk between us. 'Take this with a litre of water before you go to sleep tonight.'

I slip it into my jacket pocket.

From a drawer he pulls out a sheet of paper. 'You need to sign,' he says, placing crosses on it. 'Here, here and here.'

I pick up the pen. 'Anything, I'll sign anything.' This time I'm going to get it right, and ask Jennifer to the prom before Tom does.

Not Waving

A four-year-old child is too heavy for a six-year-old to drag from a pond. I tried, and failed, and by the time I summoned the grown-ups from the patio, it was too late.

My parents want me to keep up my swimming as I've shown such a knack for it. But it was this knack – cockiness, in hindsight – that made me think I could rescue him.

I have no memory of a time when I couldn't swim. I had no idea that other people couldn't.
It was a game, and I was Superman.

He laughed as he hit the surface.

Blink

'Angela?' I lean over the partition.

She blinks once before looking up from her computer. 'Hi, Derek.'

'I'm leaving.'

'Oh, right. See you on Monday.'

'No, I've got a new job. I won't be back.'

She blinks three times. 'But?'

'But?'

'But you can't.'

'I can't? What do you mean?' My heart clacks as quickly as the keys on the computers around me.

'Nothing. Ignore me. Good luck.'

'Thank you. I… uh… no, nothing. Take care.'

She nods. 'You too.'

I walk away, turning back only once, to see her blinking rapidly whilst looking out at the early evening sky.

In Dreams

I used to dream that you'd left me.

I'd cheated; or done some other unthinkable (and unforgiveable) thing, and I'd wake feeling so ashamed.

But then I started dreaming that I left you.

No particular reason, I just move all my clothes, pile by pile, into matching suitcases, and I leave. Every time the same. I wake from those dreams and catch my breath, like I've been running.

You reach for my hand and squeeze it, each time a little tighter. 'Everything ok?'

I nod, not trusting my voice and gaze at the bags stashed on top of the wardrobe.

Outsiders

Every year or so my wife takes up with another man. There are tell-tale signs: she hums, sways her hips while cooking.

'Bumped into [insert name] today,' she'll say, all casual. 'You know the guy who [insert something]. Well, we [insert activity].'

'Oh yeah?' I keep it light, but I know where this is heading.

Over time there'll be less humming, less hip swaying, fewer mentions, and then tears and early nights. That's how I'll know this one's over.

Then I hold her, remind her who really loves her, dreading that next time, she'll find someone who loves her back.

Good Advice

'Penny.' Susan held her daughter at arm's length. 'I want you to promise me you'll not do anything stupid.'

Somehow Penny's face looked younger with make-up on. 'Of course I won't.'

'I know you think Scott's 'Mr Right', but you're only sixteen. You've got your whole life ahead of you.' Susan followed Penny down the stairs. 'I don't want you to–'

'Make the same mistakes you did.' Penny looked up at her mother. 'I know. I won't.'

Susan stood by the window long after Penny had gone. She thought about her own mother's words, words that had been ignored.

On Repeat

She hands me the baby like I haven't just done an 18-hour shift and she says, 'I just need five minutes,' but she's ten, then twenty, and because I'm worried if I sit down, I'll fall asleep and drop the baby, I'm pacing, and thinking about how much longer I can do this, not just the pacing, but life; long shifts day after day, girlfriend who's tired and depressed, and a baby who neither of us know how to look after; then there she is and the baby's fallen asleep in my arms and for just one minute everything's ok.

Money Talks

'The *tax*, man! It was killing my lifestyle. I simply couldn't afford to live here,' Matt Butler says, sipping his third latte (the first two rejected: too milky, too coffee-y). 'Tough times.'

'You know what's really tough, Mr Butler?' I say, pen suspended. 'Not being able to pay the rent, feed your kids, or buy them new shoes. Working for a paper that's making people redundant. Dreading it's your turn next. *Those* are tough times.'

He stares at me.

He could get me sacked.

He could help.

'Wow. Awful,' he says. 'Can't get a decent Sunday roast in Gibraltar, either.'

Winning Numbers

In the first interview, I was a gabbling fool and could just about string a sentence together, saying how overjoyed I was.

A month later, I did another interview and this time I was more composed, feeling confident in my new clothes; my hair and make-up professionally done. I talked about how it had enriched my life, how I'd seen people I hadn't seen for years, how I felt I could do good and finally fulfil my potential.

After six months I gave my final interview. I told them all the money had gone. No more enrichment, no more potential.

Too Many Words

There's a language called Taki Taki that only has two hundred and forty-one words.

I think of the words that probably exist: *mother, father, son, daughter, baby. Love, hate. Birth, death.*

I think about the words that most likely don't exist: *anxiety, depression, loneliness; targets, stress, performance review, written warning.*

If there is a word for job, it might actually mean nourishment, or caring. Not sitting at a desk, staring at a screen, waiting for screamed instructions from your boss.

And if there is a word for path, it does not mean career path, but the way that leads home.

Karma

I never set out to be the other woman.

When Paul and I first met, we were barely adults, still in the fresh excitement of youth. The second time, it was quite by chance – neither of us lived near Whitstable beach, and I excused my decision by seeing it as fate.

I knew he was married, but I was lonely, and believed him when he said that he was too. Our calls and texts snowballed from every week, to every day, then we started meeting up.

Now I'm a different kind of lonely, living on the leftovers of his life.

Candy Floss

It was just a perfect day: rides, laughter, fun, candy floss. Melanie, like me, loved the funfair.

She was there, right there, walking next to me – until she wasn't.

I pushed the panic down, where it sat like a heavy lump in my stomach, and ran through the assault of lights and noises calling, shouting, screaming her name.

The police searched for hours, until stars burst into the darkening sky in lazy clusters, and the search continued for days after, but she was gone.

Every year I come back, searching every face for a trace of her, an older her.

Potluck Shopping

I tell the kids it's a game called Potluck Shopping as we unpack the two bags of tins, boxes and packets, lining them up on the kitchen counter in size order.

Earlier, in the church hall, I battled between gratitude and shame. Thank god the kids were at school and didn't have to watch me queue for handouts from complete strangers.

My mind starts calculating how many meals I can make. Gone are the days I could savour food, or even taste it. Now I just force my body to swallow it so I can function for one more day.

Birthing

'Elspeth,' Granny says, 'it's time for lunch.'

'Shh!' I say, 'Mummy Doll is having a little lie down.'

Granny pokes her head into the conservatory and whispers, 'Five more minutes then,' and goes back into the kitchen. Daddy built this conservatory because we needed more space, but the only thing that's in it is my doll's house.

Mummy Doll said she was sleeping, but her eyes are still open. Little Girl Doll tiptoes up to the bed. 'Can you read me a story?'

'No. Not now.'

Little Girl Doll kicks the empty cot as she stomps out of the bedroom.

Awakening

She plonks herself onto a chair and eats cereal as if nothing's changed. She thinks I don't know, but she reeks of it (and not just figuratively): sex.

There's dew on the grass outside and the morning sun is weak, but I get up and start opening all the windows.

'Mum,' she says, pulling her school blazer across her chest. 'It's freezing.'

She shouldn't complain about being cold. Her young, lithe body is still warm from his touch. He's a nice boy, they're in love, they're legal (*thank God*). I don't disapprove, not entirely, but still, I can't bear it.

Reckoning

Elspeth tugs at her school skirt as she walks into the conservatory. The hot, thick air makes her nauseous. Like most things these days.

'Mum,' she says.

Her mother continues reading the newspaper. 'Hmm?'

A bird dropping splats loudly onto the glass roof and they look up. 'Oh,' Mum says, dropping the paper, nose wrinkling.

'Shit.' Elspeth stifles a giggle.

'It's not funny! Those windows were only cleaned yesterday.'

Elspeth doubles over, holding her stomach, laughing. She snorts, something that takes her by surprise, chokes and her laughter curdles.

'What is it, darling?' Mum asks.

Elspeth sobs. 'Oh, Mum–'

The Pupa Stage in the Lifecycle of Audrey Brown

Audrey dyed her hair, learned to do a chignon and got coloured lenses. She took elocution lessons every Saturday with Miss Pinkerton. To stay slim, she ate almost nothing, went to the gym every day, and took dancing lessons once a week.

The NHS was unconvinced of her need for a breast reduction, so she went private.

Under anaesthetic, she dreamt that the real Audrey told her she was beautiful, *just beautiful – perfect, so natural.*

Her tears didn't go unnoticed, but they were assumed to be merely a harmless side effect, not important enough to be recorded in her notes.

AUTUMN

Empty Nest

My hand shakes as I unlock the front door. An unfamiliar silence greets me. On the living room floor a wooden train track lies abandoned, on the sofa several picture books.

A ray of light points at the photo hanging above the fireplace. It is of me, Paul and our three children; traces of family etched into their similar, but distinct faces.

Today is the first day that all of them are at school. People said I would feel lost, but the opposite is true. For a couple of hours I'm not a wife, not a mother.

I'm just me.

Be Prepared

Dad spends most of his time in the garden dressed as a rabbit. His fluffy tail bobs and his long ears flop as he tends to his vegetable patch (which only grows carrots).

Ralph leans over the side of the top bunk. 'Listen Tommy, when you start school tomorrow, kids are gonna tell you that Dad's gone funny.'

There's nothing funny about our dad.

'You just tell 'em he's only like this—'

'Because of the war.' I've heard Mum say this threehundredsixtymilliontwelve times already.

'Just be prepared,' Ralph says.

I hate them already. I shiver under the thin blanket.

The Daily Shop

Sainsbury's is a twelve minute drive, fourteen when the lights are red.

It's drizzling, so I do a walk-run to the store entrance. I imagine complaining to the security guard about the weather, but he doesn't look up as I walk past. I get a trolley and realise I've forgotten my list. Doesn't matter. Bananas are always good. Milk. Bread. Need a couple of bulky items too, otherwise they'll send me to a self-service checkout. I don't want to serve myself. I want someone to talk to, even if it's only about the weather. Before my twelve minute drive home.

Alternate Weekends

'How was your weekend with Daddy?'

Chloe pushes past me into the living room.

'Wellies off the sofa, Chloe.'

'No.'

I count to three and ask again.

'There was a strange woman there,' she says.

'Oh?'

'Daddy said I had to be nice to her.'

'Were you?'

'No.'

Inwardly I smile at my daughter's defiance, but know that's not the right thing to do. 'Maybe next time,' I say, still unsure how Rhys and I have ended up like this. I sit next to her and she crawls onto my lap, wellies banging my shins.

'Read me a story, Mummy?'

How the Camera Lies

She sits next to him on that sofa, the one they'd picked up for next to nothing at a flea market and said was just for now, but which they've ended up keeping for years. His arm is across her shoulders, a beer bottle resting against her upper arm. His head is thrown back, mouth open, looking as if laughter is spilling out, filling the room. She's smiling, eyes cast down.

The photo doesn't show that she is smiling because she must; that she is next to him because she owes him; that she can't leave, because he'd find her.

Autumn Colours

Autumn is finally here. It's cold, but bright, and I walk to the hairdressers with my hands in my pockets, chin tucked into my scarf.

My hair is pulled back into a ponytail, a style I know doesn't particularly suit me. As I walk, I look at all the other women and wonder if their hair would suit me better. Today I'm determined to go for something different. Something new. And daring.

'Morning, Sarah,' my hairdresser says. 'Just the usual trim, is it?'

I hover on the precipice of doing something different. And falter.

I force a smile, and nod.

Cat and Mouse

Nancy is tidying in the kitchen when the bell rings. That's odd, she thinks, remembering hanging up the 'closed' sign at six o'clock and locking the door.

She walks into the shop, wiping her hands on her apron.

'Hello, Nancy.'

He hasn't changed, not really, since she last saw him.

'Long time, no see.'

She exhales. 'Yes.'

'I'm impressed. You always said you wanted to open a café by the sea and here you are. The Kite.' He points at the sign above the door. 'Nice name.'

'Thanks.'

'Surely you always knew I'd catch up with you in the end?'

Housewife 500

'Claim number?'

'34675.'

'How can I help?'

'I'd like a refund.'

'May I ask why?'

'On the ad it said she could do all household chores, but she only cooks two different dishes, her washing up is patchy, and my shirts look more creased after she's ironed them.'

'Right. And, um, other services?'

'No complaints there. Although, actually, it's less and less often.'

'I see you have quite an old model. Have you thought about trading her in? The new Housewife 500 is very popular.'

'Okay, I'll try that.'

'Great. Your new wife will be with you tomorrow at noon.'

Celebrity Crush

We're doing that thing that new lovers do, of sharing everything with each other, when you tell me who your celebrity crush is.

'Really?' I say, when what I'm thinking is: but I look nothing like her.

I show the hairdresser a magazine picture and ask her to dye my hair. I start wearing more make-up and I paint my nails. I even get coloured contacts. But try as I might, I can't make my lithe frame curvy.

We are watching TV and she comes on.

'Oh! I say, look it's your favourite woman!'

'Who?' you ask, and change channels.

A Life Half-Lived

We all live in fear of Ted's van, its backdoor like the cavernous mouth of an animal with an insatiable appetite, feeding on the things we can no longer afford.

I was still asleep this morning when I heard its growl, ever louder, roaring up the cul-de-sac. I leapt out of bed and dragged the kids from theirs.

'Get up,' I hissed, 'Now!' and pushed them up the ladder into the loft. I scrambled up behind them, pulling the hatch shut as I heard the first bangs on the door.

Wonder what they'll take this time. There's hardly anything left.

Mrs Potter

'She wore a huge pink bow in her hair,' my mother says into the telephone, loud enough for me to hear. 'Most inappropriate for a grown woman.'

Lunch didn't go well. Suzie was late. Only by five minutes, but Mother was already huffing and puffing. Suzie had brought chocolates, but the 'cheap kind' and when she said, 'It's lovely to meet you, Barbara,' Mother said, 'It's Mrs Potter to you.'

I leave to find Suzie, imagining Mother's tight grip on the phone, her puckered lips opening and closing like a fish, the tinny voice of her friend filling the hallway.

A Storm in an Hourglass

Dr Li stands up as I enter the room, wearing her best 'I'm sorry there's nothing we can do' look behind new black-rimmed glasses.

I sit. 'Just tell me how long I've got.'

'I'm so sorry,' she says. 'It's always hard to predict, but I'd estimate six to twelve months.'

'At least I'll get one more Christmas,' I say, standing.

'The nurse, outside, has leaflets,' she says.

I laugh, but it morphs into a bark, a growl. 'I think we're a bit beyond leaflets, don't you?'

For the rest of the day I worry about whether I upset Dr Li.

Flying Solo

I'd never feel alone again, that's what I thought. I had the tests, found a suitable match, went through the (sometimes painful) procedures and then there was life. Heart beating, organs growing, limbs moving.

People kept telling me I was 'Oh so brave!'

I smiled and nodded, thinking that being a mother is 'Oh so natural!'

But only weeks after Eva was born, I started feeling significantly less brave. I was tired, oh so tired. I staggered through the days and spent nights rocking a screaming baby. I wanted to scream too.

I've never felt so lonely in my life.

Buried Secrets

When we found a body under the conservatory, my husband and I disagreed on what to do.

'We should call the police,' I said, hands shaking.

He pressed a cup of sweet tea into my hands. Watched me take the first sip. 'No. No, I don't think we should get anyone involved.'

I finished the tea and put the cup down. 'Ultimately, it's your decision. I'll go with what you want.' I'd calmed down a bit.

The thing is, I suppose, that we inherited the house from his parents. His dad, actually, who's in a home. His mum is dead.

Life Goes On

Unable to cope with the thought of people's pitying looks, I phoned friends and told them Neil was dead.

The following day people started arriving, armed with sympathetic smiles, meals and homemade cakes. I wore black, I smiled a lot, I cried occasionally. I was a grateful widow, so many kind people, so much delicious food; I had to buy another freezer.

Then, it stopped.

'I'd expected the attention to wane,' I said to my sister, when she finally picked up, 'but perhaps not quite so quickly.'

'The thing is,' she said, 'we've all been invited to his housewarming party.'

Don't Look Ahead

You spot her, but keep on walking, hoping she won't see you.

She trips, falls, and stays on the wet cobbles.

You sigh, and walk over to your Older Self. 'Get up,' you hiss.

'I can't,' she says.

'Of course you can.'

She looks at you, and her face is no longer an almost-reflection of yours; it's old, sad.

'What's wrong?' you ask.

'I don't know. On paper, I've got everything I ever wanted, yet I still feel... lost.'

You don't understand. You thought everything was on track.

'Come on,' you say, putting your arm around her. 'I've got you.'

Eeny Meeny

We spend Saturdays in the library because it's warmer than the bedsit. It is here that Mum tells me how she chose.

'I chose two cards from the deck: the queen of hearts and the king of diamonds, I shuffled them, and then picked one.'

My twin brother went into foster care.

'I couldn't cope with both of you,' Mum says.

Or even one, I think.

He's adopted now, living in a three-bedroomed semi that reeks of fake lemon.

She doesn't tell me whether the card she drew was for the child she kept, or the one she gave away.

Five Digit Pin

I stare at the Blockbuster card the old man's given me.

'Put it in the machine, son,' he says, like I'm the one losing the plot. My boss appears from the storeroom and slots in the card. With a shaking forefinger the old man types in a five-digit pin number.

I pack his milk, bread, and eggs into a bag.

'All done, Mr Jacobson,' my boss says. 'Need a hand getting home?'

'No, thank you.'

We watch him totter down the road.

My boss scrunches up the receipt and throws it away.

'What?' I ask. 'Why?'

He shrugs. 'Just because.'

Selective Hearing

'So,' he says, 'what are you doing later? Put on your glad rags and join me.'

As the Tube snakes through the tunnels, Zadie smooths down her berry blue skirt and thinks about him: his deep voice, infectious laughter, and how listening to him always cheers her up.

She's waiting outside the studio, crunching mints to hide the nervous cigarette smell, when he emerges, blinking in the early evening sun. He slips on a pair of sunglasses.

'Gary?' She gives him a little wave.

He smiles and saunters over. 'Want an autograph, love?'

He's not as tall as she'd imagined.

Beneath the Surface

When the lake is so still that it mirrors the sky, she slips in.

On land, she is a wife, mother, daughter; a sister, friend, colleague. Beneath the surface, she is no one. And she loves that.

Submerged, she weaves through the reeds, stirring up silt. As long as the water is restless, she can remain.

She wants to stay, but knows she can't. The endless movement would be too much for her here, she has lost the knack.

Long ago, she left the water. She chose a different life, land-locked, and it is to this life she must return.

Mercy

Killing someone isn't easy.

Shooting: where to get a gun?
Knife: messy.
Drug poisoning: can be traced in the blood.
Alcohol poisoning: ditto.
Strangulation: obvious.
What does that leave? Pillow over face. Asphyxiation, basically.

I've watched crime programmes. I know it's not fool-proof. I made him wear gloves so if he scratched me my DNA wouldn't be under his nails. I wore gloves too.

He made me promise not to stop, no matter what, not even if he told me to. So I didn't; because I would do anything for him.

But his muffled cries haunt me day and night.

Just Ask

'Mum? You there?' The letterbox slams shut.

'Coming.' I clatter down the stairs, pulling my dressing gown on.

I open the door to find him sitting on the doorstep, looking at me with a big grin on his face. For a second, I can see the boy in him. And then he's the man again, falling in and dropping himself onto a kitchen chair.

'You're high,' I say, filling the kettle. 'High as a kite.' I make a pot of tea knowing I won't sleep again tonight and wait for the inevitable.

'I need to borrow some money,' he says.

Leap Year

I'd almost given up on finding true love when I found Natalya, or she found me, I should say. And I'm totally fine with that. More than fine. I'm not one of those male chauvinist pigs stuck in the last century. Women are allowed to be forward, ask men out, propose even – although I've got my proposal all planned out, so I hope she doesn't beat me to it.

We're meeting for the first time next month. She just needs some money to buy the plane tickets and then we'll be together at long last. And honestly, I can't wait.

Conversion

My husband is moving his new girlfriend in.

'What's wrong?' I asked, when we were on holiday a couple of months ago. 'You've been grumpy all week.'

'I'm so sorry, I'm in love with someone else.'

'Right,' I said. 'Right.' An affair is one thing, love is something else.

Since we got home, my husband has converted the garage into a bedsit for them, and we've drawn up a rota for using the facilities.

I'm hiding in what was the marital bedroom. I've yet to see her, but the sounds of them together slither in, coil around me, and bite.

Support Network

I look up at the baby's cries. The mother is rocking the pram with one hand and clutching the shopping basket in the other. She's stained and rumpled, and she's got bags on her bags, as my nan would say.

'Here you go, love,' I say, adding a copy of *The New Mother's Handbook* to her bread, milk, chocolate and nappies. 'Complementary.'

I know first-hand that she won't read it, not until she's desperate, that is.

On the first page of the slim book is written *you are doing the best you can.*

The rest of the book is blank.